D1014019

SPACE ESCAPE!

Story concept:
Rafaił Katsuł
Concept and design:
AMEET STUDIO Sp. z o. o.

ISBN 978-0-545-52947-1

12 11 10 9 8 7 6 5 4 3 2   13 14 15 16 17 18/0
Printed in the U.S.A.   40
This edition first printing, February 2013

SCHOLASTIC INC.

CHAPTER 1

THE FIRST-TIME PILOT!

THE SPACE STATION IN LEGO® CITY.

UH-OH. WHERE'S MARK?

WE CAN'T HAVE A TEST FLIGHT FOR THE SPACE SHUTTLE IF THE MAIN PILOT ISN'T HERE. WHERE'D HE DISAPPEAR TO?!

HEE, HEE, HEE...

Handsome Hank, a crook with a long criminal record, rubbed his hands with glee and ran to the van he had stolen that morning. He opened the back door with a smile.

"So!" He smirked at astronaut Mark, who was lying in the back of the van, tied up with rope. "Are you comfy?"

"You'll never get away with this!" cried Mark, struggling to free himself.

"Stop squirming," Hank replied coolly. "No one will even notice you're missing."

I'M SURE THEY'RE ALREADY LOOKING FOR ME! I'M THE MAIN PILOT.

TODAY IT'LL BE ME. MY DREAM OF BECOMING AN ASTRONAUT WILL FINALLY COME TRUE!

Hank could already see himself in space. So far everything had gone according to plan.

Hank, disguised in Mark's suit, walked toward the base. Soon his dream would come true! He'd fly all the way to the stars! His thoughts were interrupted by the shout of the angry commander.

"Mark! Where have you been? You're late again!"

Hank was caught off-guard.

"Ahh, s-s-sorry, Commander," he stammered, saluting nervously. "I just—"

DON'T YOU "COMMANDER" ME! GET TO THE ROCKET! HURRY!

UH... YES, SIR!

THAT WAS EASIER THAN STEALING LETTUCE FROM A SNAIL.

The space shuttle began to shake. Handsome Hank held on tight to the controls.

3 . . . 2 . . . 1 . . .

LIFTOFF!

Flames leaped out of the engines. . . .

"Something's wrong!" said the flight controller at the command station.

"One of the engines has too much reverse thrust. Mark can't get airborne . . . Oh, no!"

Then the shuttle leaned sideways, crashed onto the asphalt, and took off at full speed toward the city.

HELPPPPP!

Hank couldn't control the shuttle. No matter what he did, the vehicle wouldn't budge.

"Stop, Mark!" shouted the onboard radio.

"How?" Hank panicked.

He frantically pushed a big red button in the middle of the control panel. The vehicle lurched. . . .

Hank didn't know that when he pushed the button, he disconnected the main fuel tank and the side booster rockets, which scooted in all directions. The shuttle was flying, but only a few feet over the ground.

Figuring that the rocket was finally taking off, Hank leaped for joy. He smashed his head so hard against the ceiling of the cockpit that he not only saw stars, but also comets and planets.

"Oooh . . . I'm . . . in . . . space. . . . " he said. He didn't realize that the rocket was flying along the main street of the city, just over the treetops, which were catching fire.

He also didn't notice the police helicopters, which had captured his vehicle with grappling hooks.

"HQ, we've got him!" a policeman reported. "We'll deliver this lost property to the spaceport."

Moments later, still a little stunned and not suspecting anything, Hank climbed out of the shuttle.

But before Handsome Hank could make peace with the "Martians," they grabbed his arms and slapped handcuffs on him.

"You mean I wasn't in space?" Hank asked in disappointment as he climbed into the police van. "I never took off?"

"Fortunately not," Mark replied. "But you can keep the spacesuit. It'll come in handy because it's mighty cold in a jail cell."

"It's not fair," cried Hank. "I just wanted to fly in space!"

"And you almost made it," said the driver of the police van. "Now you're rocketing off to a place called jail!"

CHAPTER 2

LOOK OUT—A TREE!

It was a beautiful day in LEGO City! Fireman Archer stretched peacefully on the seat of the fire engine. No burning buildings or accidental fires – or even any cats up trees to rescue! His buddy from the firehouse, Officer Brand, pulled out a thermos of hot chocolate.

"Drink cocoa when it's hot . . ." Brand began.

". . . and you won't have to work a lot!" joked Archer.

Suddenly, he froze.

DO YOU SEE WHAT I SEE?!

An unusual vehicle flew through the sky in front of the firemen. Brand was stunned. "What was that?" he asked. "It-it's a spaceship!" Archer stammered.

HQ, A ROCKET OVER THE CITY IS SETTING TREES ON FIRE. WE'RE OFF TO HELP! OVER AND OUT!

The flames quickly spread to more trees, but the firemen bravely fought the fire. A few minutes later, the only tree left to put out was a giant oak. It blazed like a torch and leaned dangerously toward the buildings.

OH, NO! LOOK AT THAT OAK!

WE'LL PUT IT OUT NOW.

BUT IT'S CRACKING! SOON IT'LL FALL ON THE BUILDING!

KRRR!

QUICK! YOU PUT OUT THE FIRE, AND I'LL...

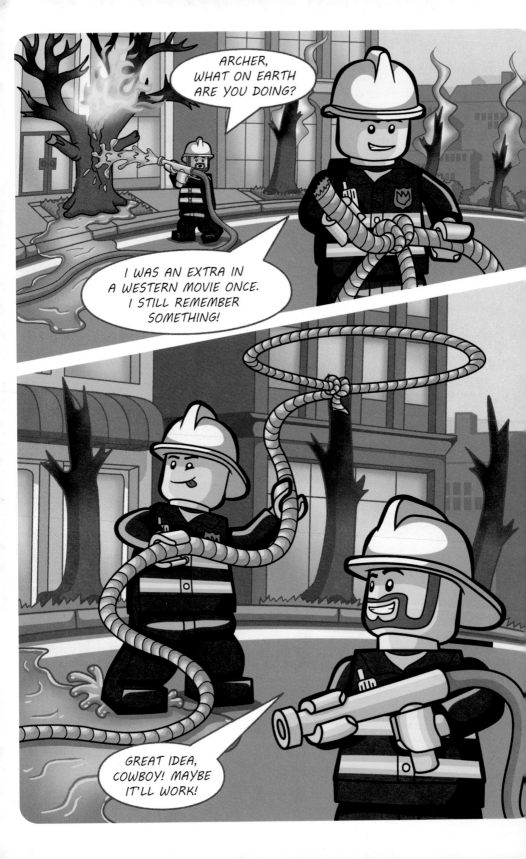

Archer tossed the lasso and tightened its grip around a sturdy branch. The fireman braced himself with his feet and pulled on the rope. *Come on, tree!* he thought, huffing and puffing.

WHAT IF THE ROPE DOESN'T HOLD?

HA 7208

I KNOW WHAT TO DO!

Archer was so focused on holding the tree in place that he didn't see that Officer Brand had also found a solution. Instead of a rope, Brand grabbed a fire hose. He spun it overhead and tossed it toward the thickest branch of the oak, and then he raced back to the fire engine.

Brand stepped on the gas, and the fire engine roared to life. The fire hose tightened as he tried to pull the tree away from the building.

Archer couldn't hear the warning over the fire truck's sirens. He was still trying to hold the tree back from falling on the building. His work was even harder because the ground all around him had turned to mud when they had sprayed water to put out the fires.

Archer finally slipped and landed softly in the mud. Meanwhile, Brand stepped even harder on the gas. The mighty tree began to pull away from the building and lean toward the fireman.

The oak came crashing down into the mud. Archer looked up and blinked in amazement. Right next to his face was the burned tree.

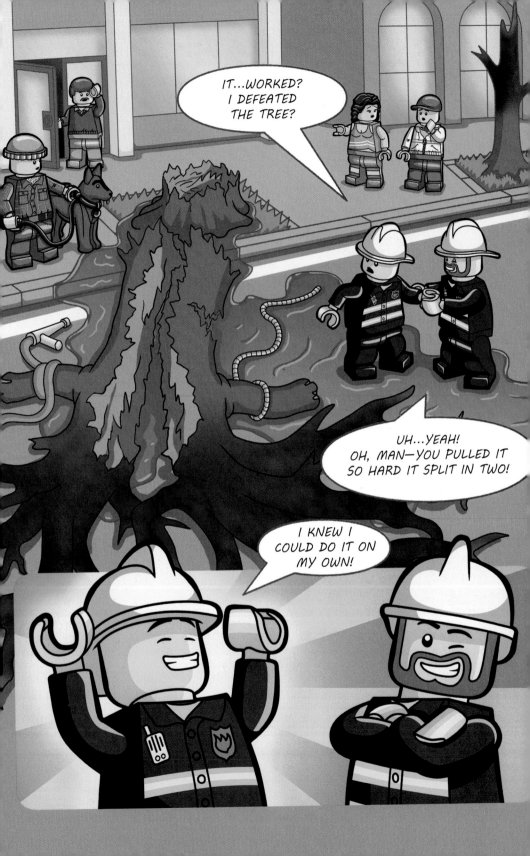

CHAPTER 3

THE GREAT ESCAPE

Handsome Hank, the first thief to try and steal a spaceship, was riding off to jail in the armored police van. Only moments ago, he had been sitting at the controls of the rocket and had almost conquered the cosmos.
Now, furious, he clenched his handcuffed fists.

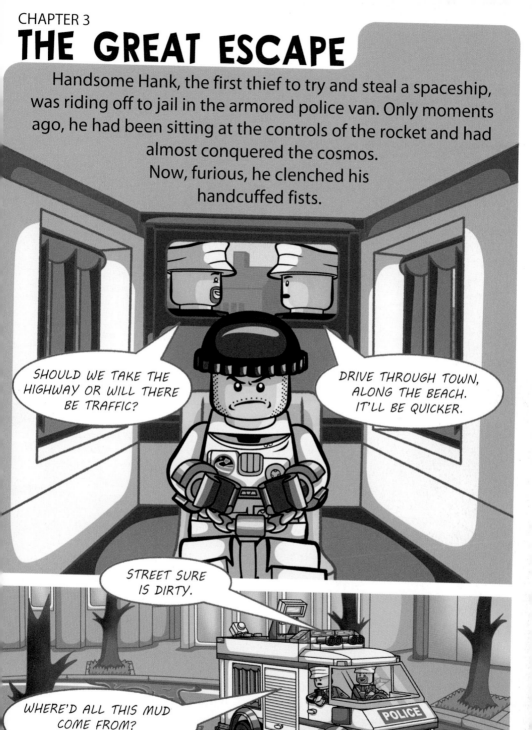

The policemen were driving along when suddenly the vehicle lost control. The tires slipped on the wet, muddy surface. The driver tried to stop the police van, but the vehicle veered off the road, crashed into the sea, and began to sink.

Just then the two policemen remembered that they had a very important passenger traveling with them. They rushed toward the police van. When they looked inside they were shocked. "Oh, no!" they both cried. "Poor Hank!"

What the police didn't know was Handsome Hank was good at holding his breath. When the police van drove into the ocean, the doors opened, and Hank escaped his handcuffs. Unfortunately, he didn't get far. Hank didn't know how to swim.

With the help of a shark, Hank quickly learned how to swim.

Seeing an engineer working on a rocket launcher, Hank had an idea. He'd sneak up, steal his van, and zip off to the train station. There he'd board a train and escape from the city.

While the operator was busy entering data into the computer, Hank crept toward the vehicle without a sound. He slipped by the rocket, and was just about to jump into the van when something snagged his outfit. . . .

THE ROCKET'S ENGINES ROARED TO LIFE.

3... 2... 1...

LIFTOFF!

LIFTOFF?

Hank didn't get far, as the rocket didn't have much gas. Lucky for Hank, he made a soft landing…in a pool of jelly! *That's it for me!* thought Handsome Hank. *I'll never steal again. Yuck! I hate strawberries!* He thrashed his arms and slowly made his way up to the surface.

The first faces he saw were familiar ones—the policemen.
Police! Here? he thought.
I've got to scram! But the sticky strawberry jelly held him until the police handcuffed him once again.

Once the jelly hardened, the brave policemen called in their helicopter.

THANKS TO YOUR ROCKET, WE CAUGHT THE CROOK! I HOPE NOTHING IS BROKEN.

DON'T WORRY. JELLY MADE FOR A PERFECTLY SMOOTH LANDING.

The police helicopter slowly flew toward the police station, lifting the cube of jelly with Handsome Hank stuck inside.

ENJOY THE RIDE, HANK! IT'LL BE YOUR LAST FOR A LONG TIME.

BUT I DON'T WANT TO FLY ANYMORE! IT ALWAYS LANDS ME IN TROUBLE WITH THE LAW!

THE END